Dear Cole,

Enjoy these play

♡ Nancy Sack

PUPPIES AND POEMS

By Nancy Sack

Illustrations by Kaitlyn Fuchs

outskirts
press

Denver, Colorado

Puppies and Poems
All Rights Reserved.
Copyright © 2011 Nancy Sack
Illustrator Kaitlyn Fuchs
v2.0

Cover and Interior Illustrations by Kaitlyn Fuchs

Outskirts Press, Inc.
http://www.outskirtspress.com

ISBN: 978-1-4327-8470-6

Outskirts Press and the "OP" logo are trademarks belonging to Outskirts Press, Inc.

PRINTED IN THE UNITED STATES OF AMERICA

Party Time

Bring out the balloons
and the streamers, too
Let's have a party
'cause it's fun to do

Bring out the boom box
let's bake a cake too
we'll dance all night
'cause its fun to do

Let's have a party
a party for two

Dancing

Hop hop hop
slide slide slide

Wiggle wiggle wiggle
giggle giggle giggle

twirl twirl twirl
around and around and around

'til your head hits the ground
and the sky's upside down

More more mor

A Merry Play

We'll have a kingdom
and wear our glitter ring
we'll slay the dragon
and even save the king

The neighbors will be glad
at the end of our show
the king is safe in his castle
and the dragon had to go

A Dinosaur Ride

rode a dinosaur
climbed onto his tail
had to crawl so very far
til I finally reached his back
le was bigger than a car

I rode a dinosaur
T-Rex ran very fast
I had oodles of fun
'til the ride was done

Blueberry Picking

I went blueberry picking
with Laura, Betty, and Mama too
All day long picking berries
Now my fingers are blue

I ate so many berries
so plumpy, juicy, and sweet
My belly is bursting
They're my favorite treat

Tomorrow's Mama's going to be bakin'
Blueberry muffins, blueberry crisp, and blueberry pi
And my belly will be bursting again
oh my, oh my, oh my

Dessert

I love desserts
How about you?

chocolate ice cream
and tiramisu

Blueberry pie
and strawberry, to

I'm dreamin' of dessert
How about you?

Books

I love books

Big books
Skinny books
Fancy books

I love
to touch them
to smell them
to hug them

But most of all
I love
to read them

Swinging

Two swings in the playground
Reserved for you and me
Let's go swinging together
As high as the big oak tree

Pump pump pump pum
but don't let g
you can swing hig
and you can swing lo

Let's swing all day long
'til the sun waves good-bye
just you and me
swinging so high

The Lake

Let's go to the lake
Just you and me

Minnows and bass
Trout and perch
They swim really fast
We'll climb a white birch

We'll collect pinecone.
nuts and shiny rock.
We'll bring them home
And hide them in our sock.

Let's go to the lake
just you and me
You'll have so much fun
Swimming with me

Bubble Gum Trouble

You want to have some fun
Let's chew some bubble gum
Yum yum yum yum yum
Let's blow the bubbles one-by-one

Oops, one popped on my left thumb
another popped on my long, pointy nose
And another found its way to my chubby toe

I'm covered in bubble gum
sticky from head to toe
I know my mom will say
into the bath you go

Night Hike

Let's take a night hike
on the nature path
we'll count the stars
and even skip our evening bath

We'll hear the crickets
calling in the night
we'll see the fireflies
flickering their light

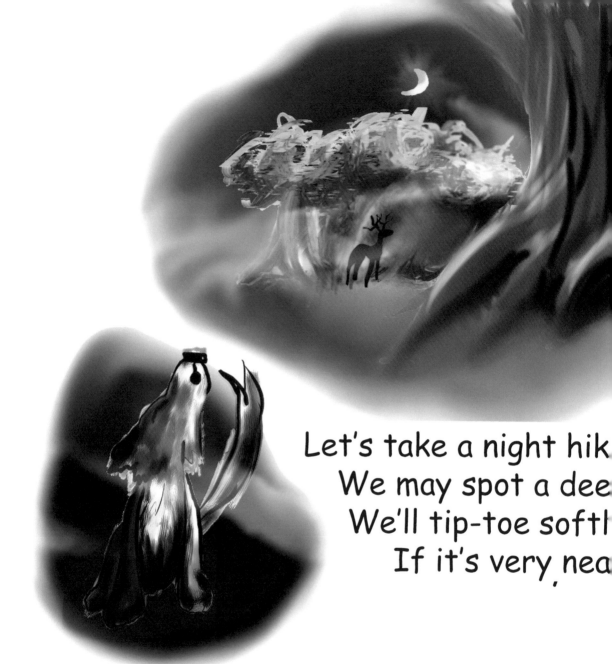

Let's take a night hik
We may spot a dee
We'll tip-toe softl
If it's very nea

Let's take a night hike
Before we go to sleep
We'll greet the Silver Moon
In the woods so very deep

Nature

I love to watch the ants
build a house of dirt

I love to watch the bees
hover and flirt

I love to watch the spide
weave a silken skir

Cookies

One cookie
two cookies
three cookies
four

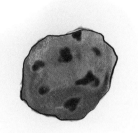

I love cookies
cookies galore

S'mores

If your life is a bore
It's time for a s'more

        You need a roaring campfire
         and a fine expert for hire

To roast a golden marshmallow
what a very nice fellow

You need a chocolate squar
on a golden graham cracke

Then comes the golden marshmallow
followed by another golden graham cracke

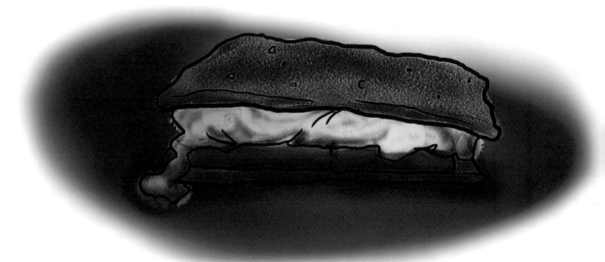

The treat will delight your inner cor
You'l be cheering s'more, s'mor

In the Pool

Come on everybody
get into the pool

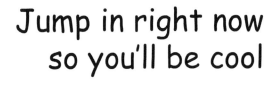

Jump in right now
so you'll be cool

Do a cannon ball
You won't be a fool

No spectators allowed
get into the pool

CPSIA information can be obtained
at www.ICGtesting.com
Printed in the USA
LVIC04n0021240617
539192LV00001B/1